Waltham For...

D0183455

My Pet Star

WALTHAM FOREST LIBRARIES
904 000 00652753

For all the carers, big and small. And my loving girl, Wren – C.A.

For Bec, my HH – R.B.

ORCHARD BOOKS

First published in Great Britain in 2019 by
The Watts Publishing Group

10 9 8 7 6 5 4 3 2 1

Text © Corrinne Averiss, 2019
Illustrations © Rosalind Beardshaw, 2019

The moral rights of the author and illustrator have
been asserted.

All rights reserved.

A CIP catalogue record for this book is available
from the British Library.

HB ISBN 978 1 408 35363 9
PB ISBN 978 1 408 35366 0

Printed and bound in China

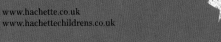

MIX
Paper from
responsible sources
FSC® C104740
FSC
www.fsc.org

Orchard Books
An imprint of Hachette Children's Group
Part of The Watts Publishing Group Limited

Carmelite House
50 Victoria Embankment
London EC4Y 0DZ

An Hachette UK Company

www.hachette.co.uk
www.hachettechildrens.co.uk

**Waltham Forest
Libraries**

904 000 00652753	
Askews & Holts	09-Aug-2019
PIC	£6.99
6105138	C

My Pet Star

Corrinne Averiss • Rosalind Beardshaw

ORCHARD

I found him underneath a tree.

Not somewhere a star should be!

He'd fallen
from his
home in space,
bumped and
tumbled,
scratched
his face.

This little star had lost his glow,
I picked him up, we hugged hello.

I took him home – he'd be my pet.

I'd be his cosmic super vet.

I cleaned off all the
leaves and soil,

fixed his arms and legs with foil,

washed his face and rubbed his back,
served up a homemade cosmic snack.

I showed him pictures in my book.

He couldn't read, but he could look.

And when I went to bed that night,
I tucked him in and held him tight.

He needed love and time and care,
and I had lots of it to share.

As days passed by, I learnt a lot

about this new-found pet I'd got.

He wouldn't wake till after dark,

He missed our ice creams in the park.

He never spoke
or made a noise.

He didn't play
with games
or toys . . .

... just smiled and shone as if to say
that being near me was OK.

Soon his sparkle got so bright,
I found it hard to sleep at night.

Instead of snoozing in my bed,
he twinkled proudly overhead.

I opened up the window wide.
Would he choose to stay inside . . . ?

Feeling strong and good as new,
into the deep, dark night he flew.

Now my star shines overhead,
where I can see him from my bed.

The brightest star who wears a smile …

...my pet star, for a little while.

More beautiful books about getting back to nature!

Along Came A Fox
Georgiana Deutsch
Cally Johnson-Isaacs

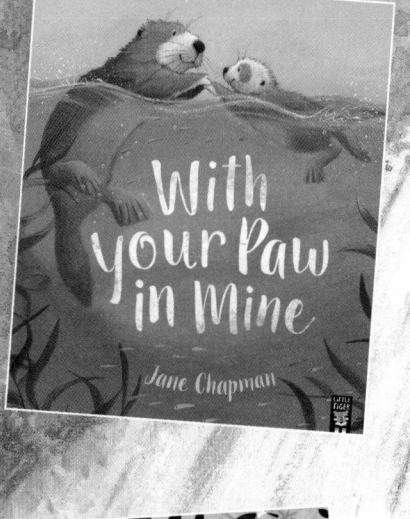

Follow Me, Little Fox
A Journey Back to Nature
Camila Correa
Sean Julian

With your Paw in Mine
Jane Chapman

When the Bees Buzzed Off!
Lula Bell
Stephen Bennett

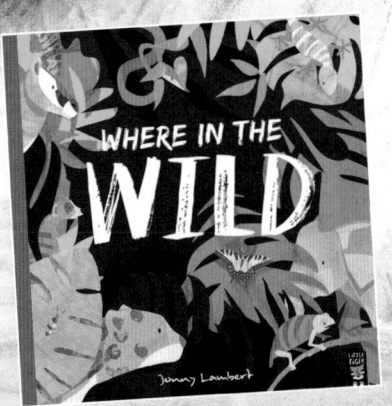

WHERE IN THE WILD
Jenny Lambert

A story of survival in our polluted oceans
Little Turtle and the Sea
Becky Davies
Jennie Poh

LITTLE TIGER

For information regarding any of the above titles or for our catalogue, please contact us:
Little Tiger Press Ltd, 1 Coda Studios, 189 Munster Road, London SW6 6AW • Tel: 020 7385 6333
E-mail: contact@littletiger.co.uk • www.littletiger.co.uk

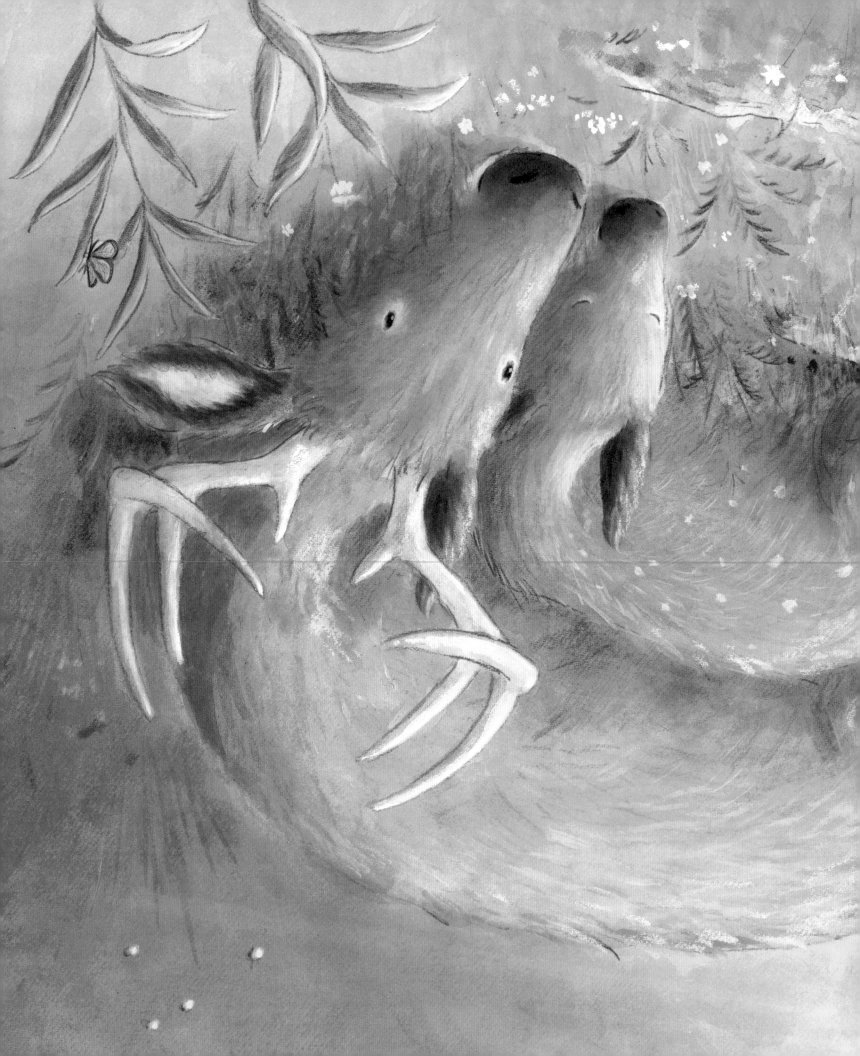

Our world will keep on turning
while we sleep the whole night through.
It's perfect and it's beautiful,
and precious — just like you.

As night draws near, let's celebrate
the wonders that we've seen,
The things we've learned together,
and the places that we've been.

Our world will always shelter us,
no matter what's in store.
Let's treat it with great kindness
so it's here forevermore.

Together, raindrops make a storm
that reaches far and wide.
Anything is possible
with others by your side.

At times, you might feel tiny,
like the smallest drop of rain.
But you can make a difference, too.
Come here and I'll explain . . . .

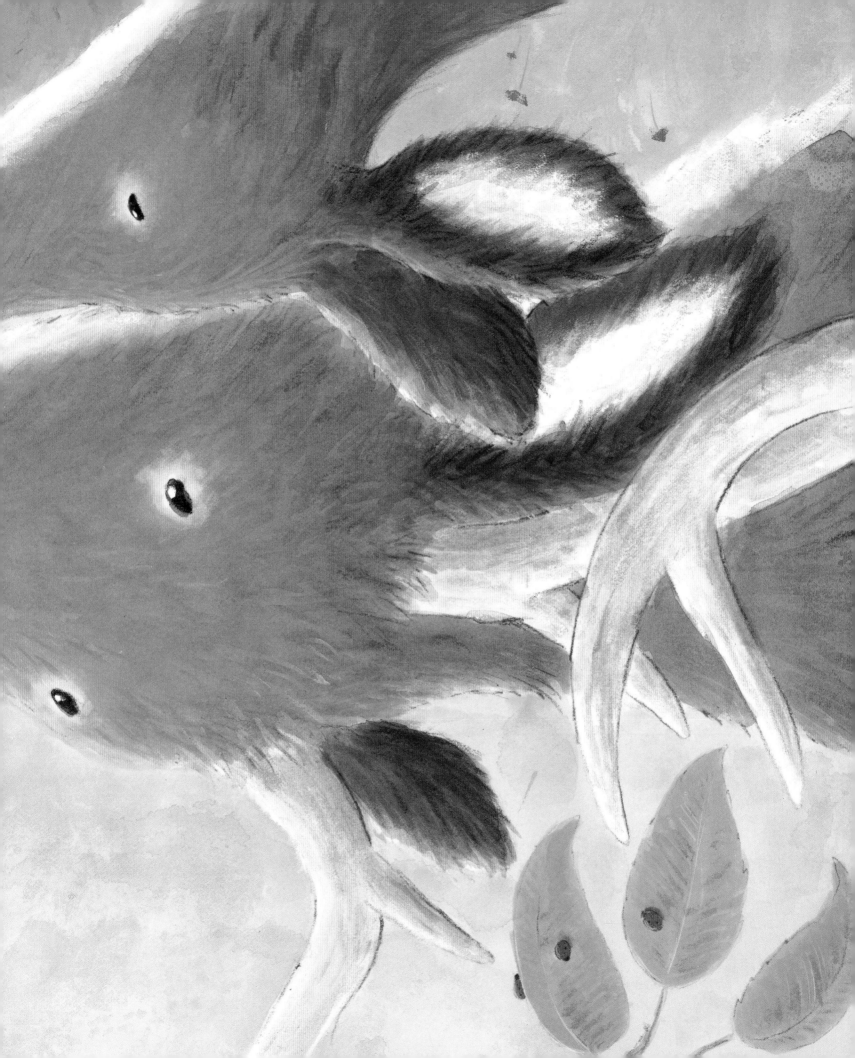

. . . For birds that soar through skies above
and whales that dive below.
It stretches out to distant places
we may never go.

This world is not just yours, or mine;
it's here for everyone —
For each and every animal
beneath the golden sun . . .

With every step, tread gently.
We must treat our world with care.
Let's only take the things we need;
there's plenty here to share.

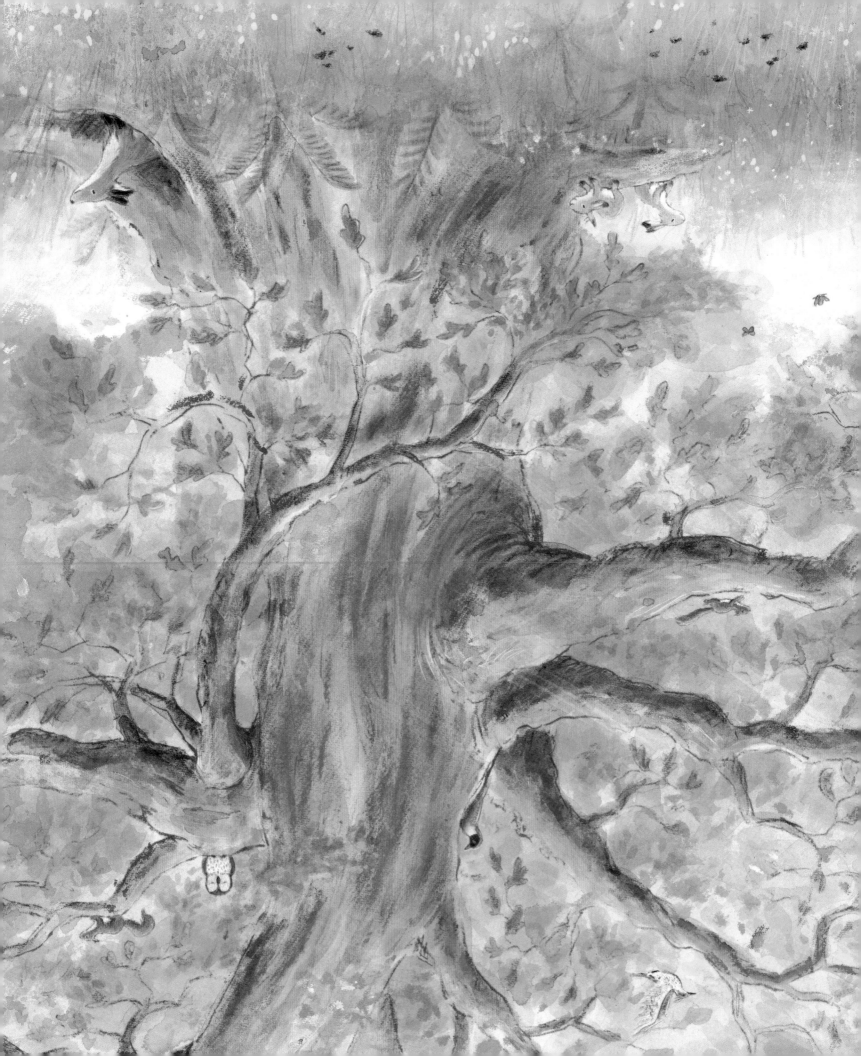

. . . a tree!

A place to eat or sit and rest
for creatures big and small.
And just as I take care of you,
this tree protects them all.

Every tiny acorn

holds a secret we can't see.

Day by day, it slowly grows,

until, at last . . .

I will show you wonders
you have never seen before.
Nature's gifts are all around —
it's your world to explore.

Time to wake up, little one —
the day is fresh and new.
It's full of precious miracles
I want to share with you.

This Is Your World

Tilly Temple   Sean Julian

LITTLE TIGER

LONDON

For Rory, Freddy, Poppy, Tilly and Evie
T T

For the Neonatal unit at the Gloucestershire Royal
Hospital. Thank you for the care, love and attention
you show the little ones – and all the big ones too!
S J

LITTLE TIGER PRESS LTD,
an imprint of the Little Tiger Group
1 Coda Studios, 189 Munster Road, London SW6 6AW
Imported into the EEA by Penguin Random House Ireland,
Morrison Chambers, 32 Nassau Street, Dublin D02 YH68
www.littletiger.co.uk

First published in the United States of America 2021
This edition published in Great Britain 2021

Text by Tilly Temple
Text copyright © Little Tiger Press Ltd 2021
Illustrations copyright © Sean Julian 2021

Sean Julian has asserted his right to be identified as the illustrator
of this work under the Copyright, Designs and Patents Act, 1988

A CIP catalogue record for this book
is available from the British Library

All rights reserved • ISBN 978-1-78881-874-2

Printed in China • LTP/2800/3753/0321

2 4 6 8 10 9 7 5 3 1

The Forest Stewardship Council® (FSC®) is an international,
non-governmental organisation dedicated to promoting responsible
management of the world's forests. FSC® operates a system of forest
certification and product labelling that allows consumers to identify
wood and wood-based products from well-managed forests.

For more information about the FSC®, please visit their website at www.fsc.org

_____

_____

_____

This Little Tiger book belongs to:

D0183791

MUNICH